AMBER OAK

MYSTERIES

Volume 1

by
Ceara Comeau

Table of Contents

The Ghost Possessed Boy

Chapter 1

One bright sunny day two brothers were on their way to school. One was named Caleb and the other was Adam. Adam was sixteen and Caleb was six, yet they both went to the same school. Adam and Caleb reached the school and Caleb ran to play with his friend Scott. Adam ran to find his friends, James and Jacob, who were also brothers.

"Hey! How's it going, Adam?" asked James.

"It's okay, but I still have to finish my history project," said Adam.

"Come on, let' go or we'll be late for class," said Jacob.

The three boys headed off for class and before they knew it, it was lunch. The three boys picked a table close to the window. While they were talking, Adam noticed a girl sitting by herself in the corner with her nose in a book.

"Who's that?" asked Adam.

"That over there is the freak of all times. She is always writing and reading. I've never seen her face out of a book, either! I think her name is Amber Oak," said James.

"That's not really nice," replied Adam.

"Unfortunately it's true and she never talks to anyone but herself. Everyone in this school thinks she's crazy!"

Jacob and James continued talking to each other but Adam seemed to be lost in thought. He couldn't help but think the guys and the whole school were wrong.

After school, Adam and Caleb were waiting for a ride when Adam noticed Amber looking at him. He looked at her and gave her a smile and she gave a curt nod back. They kept on looking at each other until Adam and Caleb's mom came. Adam waved good-bye to Amber and she stared at him as if nobody ever did that before to her. Adam got in the front seat and looked into the mirror to where Amber was but to his surprise she vanished. He turned around but she was nowhere to be seen. On the ride home Adam wondered who that girl really was, and why is she so mysterious?

Chapter 2

The next day Adam came to school looking tired. He caught up with James and Jacob and Caleb followed.

"Why don't you go play with Scott, Caleb?" suggested Adam.

Caleb looked gloomily at his brother then turned and when he did, Adam saw a round circle on his cheek.

"Hey! What'd you do to your cheek?" questioned Adam as he reached for his brother.

Caleb dodged Adam's hand and gave him a scowl and ran away.

"What was that about?" asked Jacob nervously.

"I don't really know. He wasn't like this before," replied a concerned Adam.

"Oh well maybe it's just a stage he's going through," said James.

The boys headed off when the bell rang and soon it was lunch again. The guys were eating lunch when a distressed little boy who looked like Scott came running to them.

"Scott, what's wrong?" asked Adam.

"Your brother punched me!" exclaimed Scott with tears in his eyes.

"Why?" asked Jacob.

"Because I looked at his cheek and asked him what happened," replied Scott.

Adam frowned and told Scott that it's okay and not to bother Caleb for now. After Scott ran off, Adam said, "What the heck is wrong with Caleb?"

"I think I can help with that," said a voice beside them.

The guys turned around and were shocked to see Amber right in front of them.

"What'd you say?" asked James.

"I said I could help with your problem. I know a lot about what's wrong with him," replied Amber.

"Yeah right!" exclaimed Jacob laughing.

"Hey if you don't believe me come by my house this afternoon," replied Amber, and with that she walked off.

"Maybe we should go and see Amber this afternoon," suggested Adam.

"Are you crazy?! She might kill us and nobody'll know!" exclaimed Jacob.

"Listen, Jacob! Let's go to her, she might be our only chance!"

Chapter 3

Adam was the only one who went to Amber's house. The other two boys thought Adam was crazy and decided against going with him. As soon as Adam approached the house he was shocked at how large it was. He thought to himself, "Wow, she must be rich!"

Adam went up to the door and rang the doorbell. He heard running footsteps and then Amber opened the door.

"Oh it's just you," said Amber.

"Look I'm sorry for what happened this afternoon and..."

"Say no more, Adam, I accept your apology," replied Amber with a smile.

"So you really think you'll be able to help my little brother?" asked Adam.

"Sure, follow me," she replied.

Adam followed Amber to a room that was very gloomy. As soon as he sat down Adam asked, "So you think you know what's wrong with Caleb?"

Amber stared at Adam for a while then replied, "I believe I do. What I need you to do, Adam, is to look after your brother tonight. If he goes anywhere, follow him."

Adam gave Amber a worried expression, and then said, "All right, I'll watch him."

"If you find anything interesting come and see me right away," replied Amber.

Adam nodded and headed out the door.

That night Adam lay awake in bed looking over at Caleb's bed to see what would happen. All of a sudden, Caleb got up out of bed and went out the door. Adam silently followed him.

Adam followed Caleb into the woods and he wondered, "What's Caleb going to do out here?"

Adam continued to follow Caleb and saw him go into an old little cabin in the middle of the woods. At this point Adam was terrified but he was wondering, what was his brother doing? He was about to find out. Adam quietly went to a broken window and was shocked beyond belief, not to mention scared, for Caleb wasn't alone. Right in front of him was an extremely bright bluish/white light, and Caleb was talking to it. He said, "What would you like me to do now?"

"I want you to go and find someone," replied the voice.

The next part of the conversation Adam couldn't hear. The next thing he saw was his brother nodding to the light and saying, "He will get what he deserves!"

As soon as Caleb turned around Adam gave a gasp because Caleb didn't look like himself. His eyes were glowing white. Caleb walked out of the cabin and the light inside disappeared. Adam watched his little brother walk down the path out of the woods and wondered, "What's going on and what happened to my brother?"

Chapter 4

The next day was Saturday and Adam was determined to go and see Amber. Adam banged on the door many times until Amber answered.

"Is everything okay?" she asked.

"Something extraordinary happened to Caleb last night!"

Amber smiled and replied, "Let's go to the park where it'll be quiet then you can tell me everything."

Adam nodded and they set off for the park. Once there, Adam told Amber everything.

"I see," said Amber when Adam was through, "I believe someone or rather something is using your brother for some sort of revenge."

"What?!" questioned Adam in surprise.

"Yes, and in order to prove this, you and I will go to the cabin right now."

"What? Are you crazy? What if this thing that's using Caleb is dangerous?" asked Adam.

"Who cares? Do you want your brother back or not?" Adam nodded and the two went to the little cabin in the woods. As soon as they were there Amber went inside the cabin and Adam followed.

"Seems like a normal cabin to me," said Adam.

"That's what they want you to think," replied Amber.

Adam rolled his eyes and suggested, "Why don't we search for clues as to who might be behind all this?"

"Good thinking," replied Amber.

After a long time of searching Amber spoke up and said, "Hey, I think I found something."

Adam stopped what he was doing and rushed over to Amber and saw that she was holding a black chest.

"Is it locked?" asked Adam.

"Yes," she replied.

"Arghhhh! Where's the key?" questioned Amber in an angry manner.

"Right here," answered a cold, icy voice behind them.

The teens spun around and to their surprise, stood Caleb with his pale face looking at them.

"Caleb, can you give us the key?" asked Amber.

"No, now GET OUT!!!" screamed Caleb.

"Caleb," said Adam, "listen to her, give her the key."

"I said GET OUT!!!" screamed Caleb.

The teens stood there and Caleb raised his empty hand and shot fire at them. They got the hint and ran out. Outside the cabin they turned around and were shocked to see the cabin was not on fire. They continued running to Amber's house and stopped at her back door.

"We've got to find a way to stop Caleb or he'll probably do something he's gonna regret," said Amber in between gasps.

"Yeah … but… how?" asked Adam who was also out of breath.

"I don't know… wait! Maybe we can search the little cabin in the woods on the Internet!" suggested Amber.

Adam's eyes lit up and he replied, "Perfect! My laptop is at home, I'll go get it and come back."

Amber nodded and watched Adam run back home, and she said to herself, "One way or another this thing that's taken over Caleb is going down!"

Chapter 5

When Adam returned to Amber's house they both searched on the Internet and found one article about it.

"Hey, look at this article. Here's what it says:

Tragedy in Haven Forest

This terrible tragedy happened in 1990 in Haven Forest, Wisconsin. A little boy, age seven, died in a fire that burnt the cabin. The source of the fire is unknown and remains a mystery."

"Oh man! How terrible!" exclaimed Amber.

"Maybe the little boy took over Caleb's body, and he's using Caleb to get to ..." said Adam.

"Get to the arsonist?" finished Amber.

"What?!" questioned Adam.

"Look, Adam, it says that there's some guy, named Shawn McTrevor, that's related to the little boy."

"I think we should pay this guy a visit before Caleb does."

Adam nodded and he and Amber went to find Shawn McTrevor.

The kids reached the address and knocked on the door and a man, who looked to be in his early thirties, opened the door.

"What can I do for you kids?" asked the man.

"First of all, we're not kids, we're teenagers, second of all we're looking for Shawn McTrevor," replied Amber.

"Oh! I'm sorry, and I'm Shawn McTrevor," he replied, "Please come on in."

The teens walked into Shawn's house and followed him into his living room. He motioned for them to sit down.

"Uh... Mr. McTrevor we have some questions for you," said Adam.

"Please, you can call me Shawn,"

"Okay, um can you tell us what happened to your little brother?" Amber asked.

Shawn turned pale and replied, "Well, you teens must have found out that my little brother Billy was killed in a fire but the fire was no accident, it was arson."

"Well, who was the arsonist?!" Asked Adam and Amber together.

"It... it...um... it was me," replied Shawn.

Chapter 6

Amber and Adam were horrified, but Shawn continued, "Yeah I know it sounds terrible and it is, but when I was younger I was a rebellious kid and I got into a lot of trouble. The night I set the cabin on fire my mom and dad weren't home it was just Billy and I. He got me really mad and I couldn't control myself. I was all messed up. I regret it ever since. Why do you want to know about this anyway?

"You see, Shawn, my little brother has something wrong with him. I think that your brother wants revenge on you. So his spirit is somehow controlling my brother and I overheard him saying to your brother that you'll get what you deserve."

"Well, what should we do?" asked Shawn.

"I've got an idea" said Amber, "We can sort of use you as bait and we can have you stand in front of the cabin and when Caleb comes, we can try to get rid of this spirit and put Billy to rest."

"We can try that, but what if Billy gets really angry and really does try to kill all of us?" asked Adam.

"We'll have to take our chances. Come on, let's go," replied Amber.

The teens and Shawn reached the cabin and Shawn stood in front while Adam and Amber were off in the bushes waiting. Suddenly Adam and Amber saw Caleb walking toward the cabin and stopped in front of Shawn. The teens jumped out of the bushes and ran to Shawn's side. Amber spoke up and said to Caleb, "Look, revenge isn't the answer. Shawn's really sorry about what happened and he regrets what he did. Please forgive him, he's really sorry."

Caleb looked at Shawn and Shawn said, "Billy I'm terribly sorry about what happened. Please, I beg you, forgive me."

Caleb responded to Shawn, "You are a terrible person and you deserve to be punished!!!"

Caleb got really mad and the earth started to shake, trees started falling all around them, too.

"Adam! The black chest and key, hurry go get them!" exclaimed Amber.

Adam ran inside the cabin and got the chest and ran back outside.

"I got it!" he yelled.

Amber grabbed the chest and key from him, unlocked the chest and ran toward Caleb and said, "Leave him alone! Be gone!"

Billy's spirit was lifted out of Caleb and Caleb's cheek was healed. The earthquake stopped and everything was all right once again.

"Amber!!!" yelled Adam.

Amber turned around and saw the house crash and Shawn was stuck under a timber. Amber and Adam lifted the timber off of Shawn.

"Are you okay?" asked Amber.

"Yeah, I think my leg is broken, though," replied Shawn weakly.

The teens helped Shawn back to Adam's house and Caleb walked with them not knowing what had happened. As soon as they reached the house they called an ambulance and Shawn turned himself in. Adam walked Amber home and said, "Wow! What an adventure!"

Amber nodded and said, "I hope I'll be able to help people out like this more often."

Adam replied, "I'm sure you will."

Amber wouldn't know how right Adam was until her next mystery: The Mystery in the Asylum.

The End

The Mystery in the Asylum

Chapter 1

One day two brothers were walking home from the park. Their names were James and Jacob. While they were walking they noticed an old creepy building. James, the more adventurous of the two decided to go in it.

"Wait, don't go in there!" exclaimed Jacob the oldest.

"Oh, come on! What's the worst that's gonna happen?" asked James.

Jacob looked a little unsure but went in after his brother.

The building looked old and it appeared to be an asylum of some sort. There were a lot of buildings like this in the state a while back. The oddest thing about this one was that every single item was left in its place! It looked like the doctors just left.

James and Jacob walked a bit farther on and suddenly something moved in the corner. The boys jumped when they saw two green eyes staring back at them.

"Meow"

The boys sighed in relief. It was just Emerald, their neighbor's black cat. The boys walked a little further and stumbled into a morgue. Except for the dust, it looked like someone had stepped out and would be returning any moment. They found a couple of rat skeletons and coffins but that was it.

"Jacob!! Come take a look at this coffin!" exclaimed James.

Jacob walked over to the coffin and found the weirdest saying inscribed on it. It said:

Here lies Jasmine Blair the most insane person ever to dwell in this asylum. One day she got so furious with the doctors that she made them run for their lives. After doing so she killed herself.

"Man, that's pretty bad," said Jacob.

"Yeah, it is. Hey there's a symbol above her name and it's covered with dust," said James.

James brushed off the dust and just as he did, the coffin started glowing. Then it stopped glowing and the cover slid open a crack.

"Wow! Glad that's over with!" said James.

"Don't be so sure! Look!" replied Jacob.

The boys turned around and saw the ghost of Jasmine Blaire. "Hello I'm Jasmine Blaire and I need your help"

James spoke up and asked, "Why do you need our help?"

Jasmine tuned to face James and said, "You are the ones who released me, and now that I'm free I can clear my name."

The boys looked at her in confusion. Then Jacob asked, "We thought you were insane and were going to attack us!!!"

The ghost lady laughed and said, "I would never attack you! All I ask is that you help me clear my name.

You see the problem is everyone thinks I'm insane and that I drove the doctors out of the asylum. They have the wrong girl!!!"

Jasmine started to cry. James then asked, "Well, who did drive the doctors out?"

Jasmine wiped her tears and said, "Follow me, I will show you."

A little while later, they came to a cemetery. Soon the boys found her by a tombstone. James read it aloud, "Here lies Brittany Blaire."

"You see?!" Jasmine asked, "It wasn't me who sent the doctors running for their lives, it was Brittany, my sister!!!"

"Wait a minute!" exclaimed Jacob, "So she set you up?!"

"Yes," replied Jasmine.

"Then you both know what we need to do now, said James, "we need to find a way to clear Jasmine's name!!!"

Chapter 2

While James and Jacob walked home from the cemetery James asked, "How in the world are we going to clear Jasmine's name?"

The boys thought on that for a while then James spoke up again and said, "Why don't we be detectives?"

Jacob thought about this for a moment then said, "Okay. First we need to think like detectives."

But James said, "We don't know anything about them."

Jacob was just getting into the detective spirit when his brother said that and he became sad. James thought a moment then got a great idea, "I think I know who knows a lot about being a detective."

"Who," asked Jacob?

"Don't you remember Amber Oak?" questioned James.

"Remember how she helped out Adam a couple months ago?" continued James.

"Yeah but we totally ticked her off! What makes you think she'll help us after what we said to her?" replied Jacob.

"Yeah but you never know until you try," said James.

"All right, but she's never going to talk to us," said Jacob pessimistically.

When they got to Amber's house and knocked on the door. Amber ran down the stairs to find the two boys whom she disliked the most.

"Wow! This is an unexpected and unpleasant surprise," said Amber angrily.

"Look Amber, we're really sorry for what we said. We were totally out of line," said James.

"Yeah, you were!" replied Amber.

"We really need your help and you're the only one we know that can help us. Adam says you're really good at solving paranormal mysteries," said James.

"What makes you think I'm going to help you with this? After all, you would have never asked for my help if Adam didn't." questioned Amber.

"Because we can't figure this out and you could use a little more experience if you want to be a private eye when you get older," said Jacob.

Amber gasped and asked, "How do you know about that?"

"Adam talks a lot about you, Amber," replied James.

"Fine, I can't believe that I'm saying this but... I'll help you. Come in."

Chapter 3

The boys decided to tell her everything about what they had seen and heard. When they were done Amber said nothing. After a while of thinking, Amber finally came to a decision. She decided that the best place to find out about Brittany Blaire would be at the library or on the Internet. The boys thanked her for her time, but before they left Amber advised them, "You probably want to question people who knew Brittany. Oh! Remember too, that the ghost lady could be lying to you."

Both boys laughed at her. She didn't like this and warned them "Appearances are deceiving. I'd remember that if I were you." With that she shut the door and felt very angry yet again.

The first stop on discovering the mystery was to go to the library, because not only did they have books but they also had computers. When they got to the front desk, Jacob asked the librarian if she new anything at all about Jasmine or Brittany Blaire. The woman looked at the boys as if they grew two heads with several eyeballs. Then the boys looked at each other and Jacob said to his brother, "Maybe that wasn't the best question to ask." Then James said to the woman, "Never mind, we'll find it ourselves. Thanks, anyway."

The boys split up and Jacob logged on to the Internet while James went to the books. After a while of searching Jacob called James over to the computer and said, "I've found something, but you're not going to like it!!!"

Chapter 4

"According to what it says here, Amber was right!!!" explained Jacob. "Jasmine was lying to us!"

"Why didn't we listen to her?" questioned James. "I guess the only thing to do is dig up more dirt on Jasmine. I guess we can cross off Brittany Blaire as the suspect and focus on Jasmine," said Jacob.

The boys kept searching until Jacob found something more about Brittany Blaire. He called James over and Jacob said, "Apparently this Brittany character was a kid that every parent wished to have. She was a good athlete, she was a fine artist, she loved animals of all sorts, she was an "A" student, she did extra curricular activities, and she visited the elderly. This list goes on and on about what she did, but let's type in Jasmine Blaire and see what comes up. After a few moments a screen popped up with several hundred links. Jacob scanned and scanned until he found one link titled:

"The Story of the Terror Child, Jasmine Blaire."

When the boys opened up the link they found that the author was Melanie Blaire. The boys figured that it was Jasmine and Brittany's mother. Now, the boys knew that she was dead but they figured that the Blaire's might have some surviving relatives. So they went on searching and found one distant relative whose name was Holly Oak. Then the boys got her address and James said, "Let's pay Miss Holly a visit."

With that, they thanked the librarian, who was still looking at them strangely, and walked out the door.

Chapter 5

The boys had to take a train, and then a subway in order to get to Holly Oak's house and of course they asked their parents and their parents said yes. It took them a while to get to Holly's house but eventually they got there.

"133, 134, 135, 136, 137, 138, 139…140!" counted James, "Here's her house."

Once they knocked on the door they waited and waited until they heard a loud crash and a bloody murder scream coming from the living room. The boys were a little scared at first but decided to go and investigate. When the boys got to the window they turned paler than snow. Right in front of them stood Holly and right in front of her was Jasmine Blaire only she looked different. On the side of her face was a long cut from where she killed herself and it was bleeding like crazy, her hair looked red and wild and her eyes turned a blood red, and when Jasmine began speaking her voice was deep and not as sweet as when the boys last heard her. Then she began to speak and said, "you can't run from me and you can't hide from me, either way you'll end up just like everyone else in… well, what used to be our family. Ha ha ha ha!!!"

Holly finally had the courage to speak up and replied, "You can do whatever you want to me, but I'm not the last in the family. There's one more girl who's fifteen, but you'll never find her!"

Jasmine seemed to get angrier and replied, "You know I can take your life just as easily as I did with everyone else, right? So if you don't tell me where that girl is I'll kill you!"

Holly replied solemnly, "As you wish."

Suddenly there was a great bright red light, which looked like fire. When the light was gone Jasmine disappeared and Holly fell to the floor. The boys rushed inside and ran to Holly's side, which was bleeding immensely, and her pulse was very weak but she opened her eyes and said, "Find my daughter and protect her and whatever you do don't let her out of your sight!"

The boys were startled that this complete stranger would tell them to look after her daughter. It must have been one of those things people do before they die.

Then James asked Holly, "What is your daughter's name?"

Holly replied weakly, "Her name is Am..." James felt her pulse but there was none.

"She's dead," said James.

The boys called an ambulance and the ambulance took Holly away. The boys took the long ride home and on the way Jacob asked James, "Who do you think Am is?" James thought on that for a second and said, "Aw, come on, use your head, its Amber! I think we need to see her again, but I know she's right about one thing."

"What's that?" asked Jacob."

"Appearances are deceiving!!" said James.

Chapter 6

When they got to Amber's house, they knocked on the door and Amber answered it. She asked, "What do you want now?"

The boys saw that she was obviously upset with them. James said, "You were right when you said that appearances are deceiving."

Amber smirked at his remark.

"We've got some bad news for you, but first you need to come with us," said James grabbing Amber's wrist.

"Wait, what?" asked Amber pulling her wrist out of James' grip.

"Look," said Jacob, "we can't talk about it here and now. Come with us to our old tree house. Then we'll talk."

The girl finally agreed and off they went to the tree house.

When they got there the boys started telling Amber everything that had happened. After they told her, Amber turned pale just like Holly did. Then she told them, "Okay, Holly Oak was my mom, and I am Amber Oak. My mom told me that I needed to stay with some friends when I was little, right? So I did. She didn't tell me why, but I went. She told me a lot about the asylum and even about Jasmine and the reason why you guys saw the name Brittany Blaire on the tombstone is because that was my Grandma's name and she lived with my mom until Jasmine took her then she went for my mom. Now I'm the only one left." Jacob then asked, "Why does your Aunt want to kill you and your relatives?" Amber replied, "Because she's crazy. When she was alive I remember her getting angry at nothing and when my mom found out she sent her to a doctor and he sent her to the asylum. While she was there she kept claiming that the doctors were hurting her. Then one day she got extremely angry with them and drove them out. Then she took a doctor's scalpel and killed herself. Ever since then she's tried taking revenge on my family because they put her in the asylum."

James who was being so quiet asked, "Why does she want to kill you? You didn't do anything."

Amber replied, "Your question is as good as mine! Oh! The reason why my mom said for you to keep an eye on me is because somehow you're my third cousins. I know it seems really weird, but when you told me about what's going on I decided to do some research and, well, I found out that you and I are cousins. The point is that if any of us are alone then we could all be killed!!! For some reason she's only looking for the kids now and that is us. So right now we need to figure out a way to make her move on. Another reason why no one was in the asylum ever since that day was because anyone who touched the coffin of Jasmine Blaire would release her and she would get even angrier. I also think the reason she wants us is because she thinks we might hurt her. She doesn't know you two are related to me but that's a good thing."

The three kids were thinking of ways to put Jasmine to rest until James came up with an idea. "You know the day or should I say night that Jasmine died is tomorrow. So maybe Jacob and I can call Jasmine when we're in the asylum and we can close it shut for good. Then we can call the police and they'll take her away."

Amber said, "Sounds good, but for tonight, where will I stay since we can't be alone because that will make us more vulnerable to Jasmine?"

The boys said that their parents would be glad to have her and she could sleep in the guest bedroom.

"Okay but tomorrow we'll start making more plans," she said.

Chapter 7

The next day was Saturday and the kids were ready for anything, even Jasmine. The boys went to the asylum and Amber followed far behind. When the boys got there and opened the door a strange feeling came over them. The boys figured that the only thing watching them was Jasmine so they had to be careful what they said. Then James called out, "Jasmine, Jasmine!"

Then out of the corner came a white mist, which circled the boys. Then it formed into a shape of a lady and she asked sweetly, "Have you found a way to clear my name?"

"Well, no, we haven't," said James.

Then Jasmine got mad, even madder than she was at Holly's house. Her eyes turned bloody red and her hair was wilder than before and her dress tuned red and she screamed, "That was not the right answer!!!!"

She threw them across the room, and the boys fell against the wall. Then Jacob slowly rose up and said, "What happened to you? You were so nice before!!!"

Jacob knew what her answer was; he just made small talk so Amber would have enough time. Jacob knelt down beside his brother and checked his pulse to see if he was alive and he was. He was just unconscious. Now it was just up to Jacob and Amber. Just then Jasmine spotted Amber heading for the coffin and she shot electricity at her. Amber was jolted back and Jacob saw a long deep cut on Amber's face. Now Jacob was the only one who could stop her. While Jasmine was distracted with Amber, Jacob snuck up behind her and opened the coffin. Immediately Jasmine was sucked into the coffin and Jacob pushed the cover closed. The lid automatically sealed itself. Jacob looked over at his brother and saw him regaining consciousness. Jacob helped him up and they both went over to Amber and knelt down next to her. She finally regained consciousness and sat up.

"Ugh! My head kills!!" exclaimed Amber.

"That's because Jasmine shot electricity at you and knocked you out and your head's bleeding," said James.

The three teens walked out of the asylum after calling the police to take Jasmine's coffin away and the teens went to James and Jacob's house. There Amber got her head fixed and she said to the boys, "Oh man! This is going to be a huge scar!!"

"At least it looks cool!" said Jacob with a laugh.

"Hey, Amber, think about it this way, you're a hero," said Jacob.

"What do you mean? You're the one's who discovered Jasmine," replied Amber.

"Yeah, but you're the one who knew what we were dealing with," said James with a reassuring smile.

Amber finally agreed and decided to go home. On her way home she wondered how many more mysteries there were for her to solve.

She would soon find that out in her next mystery... Amber and the Red Rug Room.

The End

Special thanks to my Dad for giving me the inspiration to write this story.

The Red Rug Room

Chapter 1

Once upon a time there were two girls named Gwen and Amber. One day Amber went over to Gwen's house. While they were playing in Gwen's room, Amber needed a bathroom break. There were several doors in Gwen's house and Amber was not sure where the bathroom was. So she picked the door on her right. When she opened it she found herself in the most beautiful part of the house. It was a room with white walls and a scarlet carpet, with twin staircases that went to the second floor. After a while Gwen wondered where Amber was so she went looking for her. Suddenly Gwen found Amber in the red rug room. She yelled out to Amber, "Amber, we're not allowed in here!"

Amber replied, "Haven't you ever wondered what was in here?" Gwen stuttered, "Yeah, sure but my mom says no."

Amber agreed not to go any further, but the rest of the day she kept wondering about the red rug room.

That night Gwen invited Amber for a sleepover. Amber was very curious about the red rug room. Amber waited until she was sure Gwen was asleep. She went into the red rug room and up one of the staircases, then glancing back quickly to make sure Gwen wasn't following her, she walked a little ways down a dark hall and then saw three doorways and stopped. "Which door should I choose?" she wondered. She decided on the middle door and she walked through. When she got through the door, she stared in awe as she looked all around the room then went back into the hall. The hall was different then the room.

She went back into the room and looked out the window and saw the ocean. She said to herself, "Where am I?"

Chapter 2

Gwen woke up and looked to where Amber slept and found she wasn't there! She knew where Amber would be. When she got to the red rug room, she ran up the other staircase and looked down the hall and noticed a door open. As she walked through the doorway she saw Amber at the window.

"Amber!" she said, "What are you doing in here? You're not supposed to be in here."

Amber responded, "So you knew about this?"

Gwen hesitated and said, "No."

Amber spoke up and said, "Where are we?"

Gwen answered, "I don't know, but I think I know who would."

"Let's go outside," said Amber.

"I don't know about this," said Gwen nervously.

"Oh! Come on," pleaded Amber.

Gwen reluctantly agreed. When they got outside they were shocked at the enormous size of the building. It looked like a mini Buckingham Palace! There were gardens and the oceans in the distance, "Why is this place in your house?" asked Amber.

"I don't know, maybe we can look around more," suggested Gwen.

Amber nodded.

They started walking around and after awhile they found a statue. The statue looked like a princess, and there was a plaque that said, "Here lies Elizabeth Wilson princess of Wales."

"Both girls looked at each other and wondered what "Princess of Wales" meant. Were they in Wales, England?

Chapter 3

They decided to keep looking in the Castle. They came to the master bedroom and found tons of books; it looked more like a library than a bedroom. So they went through the books to see if they could find anything about Elizabeth Wilson. Finally they found a book about Elizabeth, and it said that she was a princess of Wales at one time and her summer home was Wilson Castle in Freeport, Maine! She had a lot of royal subjects, but they either died or went to another castle, but the princess drowned on a ship heading to Freeport, Maine.

"She was one of the most famous princesses in England," said Amber.

"This still doesn't explain why this place is in your house!"

"Maybe someone in your family knows something about this, but the question is, who?" said Amber.

Both girls thought for a moment then Gwen spoke up and said, "I know who would know!"

"Who?" asked Amber.

"My grandfather!" she replied with an excited expression.

When the girls got through the door in the princess's room they went to find Gwen's grandfather. Finally, they found him in his study, "Grandfather," cried Gwen.

"Yes, what is it Gwen?" Her grandfather called.

"We need to ask you something," said Amber.

"Well, I'm listening," said grandfather.

"What do you know about the red rug room and the middle closed door on the second floor?"

Gwen felt happy she could let that out. Suddenly her grandfather looked deathly pale and said, "That door is closed for a reason."

Both girls looked at each other and asked why.

"Because, I made a mistake," he replied sadly.

Both girls sat patiently waiting for grandfather to keep going.

"I knew the princess, in fact she was my best friend."

The girls were in awe, but sat quietly.

"People think that she died from that boat sinking, but nobody knows how. I think the only reason the door is going into her room is because after she died a servant went to clean out her closet and found the red rug room. Now I believe that princess Elizabeth wanted someone to find out the cause of her death. I know it wasn't old age because she was sixteen years old when she died. Considering I'm too old, you girls must find out what happened. Luckily we don't have a time limit but the sooner the better."

The girls puzzled over this while thanking Grandfather and left the study to go back to the castle.

Chapter 4

When the girls finally got to the castle, Amber spoke up and said, "How do we find out how she died?"

Gwen spoke up with a scared voice, "Maybe she was murdered, but by who, and why?"

After a moment of silence Amber said, "Why don't we ask people who knew her, other than grandfather!" Gwen agreed.

They decided to tour Freeport, Maine, but the matter of transportation stood in the way.

"I know, do you have any money for a taxi ride?" asked Gwen.

"But wait," exclaimed Amber, "We don't even know what time we are in, for all we know we could be back in the early 1900's!"

Now Amber had a point. They couldn't just walk out in the street and call "Taxi!" Then Gwen had an idea, "What if we go and see if there are any people around, and then we can get an idea of how to talk and act.

The girls started off on their journey to find out what happened to Elizabeth Wilson.

The girls finally found a house. When they knocked on the door a butler answered, and asked, "Hello, what do you young ladies need?"

Amber said, "May I ask what year this is?"

The butler looked at her as if she had two heads, and said, "It is 1929 of course anyone would know that."

Both girls were shocked, they thought it was at least 1980 but no. Gwen then asked, "May I ask a question?"

The butler looked kind of annoyed, but Gwen continued, "Is Princess Elizabeth Wilson alive?"

Now it was the butler's turn to be shocked and said, "Sadly, no, she… she died last night."

Amber thought, "Good, we're not to late!"

"Thank you for your time, we really appreciate it!"

As the girls turned away the door closed behind them. Amber said to Gwen, "Well, we're the detectives now! Maybe we should ask the people that knew her, but first let's get out of these clothes and into some that fit the 20's. The girls went to a store and the storeowner felt so bad that he gave the girls free dresses, anyone they wanted. Gwen chose a green outfit while Amber chose a blue outfit. Now that they had proper clothes, people wouldn't stare at them. After thanking the owner for the clothing Amber asked him if anyone personally knew Elizabeth Wilson and where to find them. He gave them a long, long, long, list of people. Gwen said, "We've got a lot of work to do, I hope Mom doesn't expect us to come home for dinner. Maybe Grandfather will cover for us."

"Who's first on our list?" asked Amber.

"James Smith, he's a friend of Princess Elizabeth," replied Gwen.

Chapter 5

The girls went to the house of James Smith. They asked him some questions but he wasn't very helpful. The next person that was on the girls list was a girl named Rosealina. When the girls got to her house, Amber knocked on her door and a maid answered it and asked, "May I help you?"

"Yes," said Gwen. "Is Miss Rosealina here?"

"Is she expecting you?" questioned the maid.

"No, but we'd like to ask her a few questions."

The maid let the girls in and showed them to Rosealina's room. When the girls approached, they saw what looked like a figure at the window.

"Rosealina?" asked Amber.

Rosealina turned her head toward the girls with a sad expression.

"May we ask you a couple of questions?"

Rosealina nodded, yes. Amber asked, "Do you know how Elizabeth Wilson died?"

The girl replied, "umm... I don't know, I think she had some sort of disease, yes, a disease."

Amber looked doubtful and asked, "How can you get a disease instantly?"

The girl looked nervous but Amber continued on, "Was she murdered? If she was do you know who it is, or is it someone you're very close to?"

The girl gave Amber a cold stare and asked, "Don't you even dare accuse me of either keeping terrible secrets or killing my cousin! Get out of my house before I call the authorities!"

"But," began Gwen.

"Get out NOW!!!"

The girls rushed out and fell breathlessly on the grass, nearby.

The girls went to another person on their list to see if they knew anything about Miss Rosealina. The person's name was Rebecca Johnson. She was a friend of Princess Elizabeth and knew Rosealina. When they found her house they knocked on the door and a girl appeared. The girl asked, "What do you want?"

Amber politely responded, "Are you Rebecca and if you are may we ask you a couple of questions?"

"I suppose," said Rebecca with a bored tone.

Rebecca invited them into her house, and led them to the parlor, which was a beautiful shade of lavender.

"Well, what is it you wish to ask me?" the girl asked.

"What do you know about Rosealina?" asked Gwen.

"There are several things I know about Rosealina, what do you want to know?" questioned Rebecca now curious.

"Did she kill Princess Elizabeth Wilson?" Gwen continued.

Rebecca looked a bit more scared and serious then replied, "Rosealina was very jealous of Princess Elizabeth. She hated the fact that the princess was prettier and richer than her. You see, she is a Duchess, but she does have a motive, maybe you should question her?"

"Sorry, we tried that but it didn't work, she yelled at us and threatened us," said Amber.

"Well, maybe she calmed down some and now you can talk to her," suggested Rebecca.

"You might be right, let's go question her more," said Gwen.

The two girls thanked Rebecca for her time and took off again toward Rosealina's house, hoping she'd be in a better mood.

When they got to Rosealina's house, and knocked on the door Rosealina answered and exclaimed with an angry voice, "What do you want now?"

Amber spoke up and said, "What was your relationship with Princess Elizabeth Wilson?"

Rosealina got angry and said, "Excuse me? I will have you know uh... Lizzy and I are... I mean we're, never mind, you wouldn't understand."

"What wouldn't we understand? That you were so jealous of Elizabeth that you killed her?" pressed Gwen.

"I'm so sorry. I never meant to push her off the edge of the window on the second floor. I just got so angry. I tried to save her but she fell. I regret what I did but I couldn't control myself!" cried Rosealina, "Now please go away, I need to be alone."

The girls left her and waited outside then decided that later they would come and see if she was okay. After waiting for a while they knocked on the door, and the door opened.

They went to the parlor and couldn't find her. Amber took the upstairs and Gwen took the downstairs. Amber searched the whole room and top floor. Then went to Rosealina's room and had an idea. Suddenly Gwen heard a scream from the top floor. She ran upstairs and saw Amber looking very pale, pointing to the ground. Gwen looked to where Amber was pointing and saw Rosealina's crumpled, lifeless figure.

They walked back to the castle feeling very sad and went through the door leading to Gwen's house. They shut the door and went to find Gwen's grandfather.

"Hey girls, what's wrong?" asked grandfather.

The girls spilled out their story and grandfather listened.

"I'm glad you girls found out what really happened, but I'm sorry you had to find out that way. Thank you for telling me," said grandfather.

The girls left him and went back to Gwen's room, "So what now?" asked Amber.

"I don't know about you, Amber, but I've had enough of being a detective," said Gwen.

Amber smiled and said, "I don't know about me. It seems pretty fun but this might've been my last chance to solve a mystery."

"Oh I don't think so! You have an amazing talent and you should use it! My talent is filming, yours is being a detective. There probably will be many mysteries for you to solve. You just have to look for them and be ready!" said Gwen.

Amber started laughing at her but Gwen wasn't too far off.

The End

Special thanks to my cousin Gwen who inspired me to write this story.

The Skeleton's Secret

Chapter 1

A long time ago there was a girl named Amber Oak. Now Amber was different than most girls, in fact she was a tomboy. She loved gross facts and she did the weirdest things that a girl her age wouldn't do. She was a detective. She'd always try to find a mystery to solve but most of the time she'd find herself in danger. The next mystery she was about to solve she'd find out what danger really meant.

It all started on the 23rd of July. She was at her house along with her friends, Kendra, Sean, and Dylan.

"So, what do you guys want to do now?" asked Amber.

All three shrugged. Amber looked a bit disappointed. This was supposed to be the best day ever; after all she was turning sixteen.

"Do you guys want to go and play laser tag?" suggested Amber.

"Amber, we've played that five times already!" exclaimed Kendra.

Amber walked over to where an old house use to be. All that was left was an old cellar hole. She gave a loud sigh, and stomped her foot on the ground. Amber stopped suddenly which made her friends look up from pulling up the grass.

"Is something wrong?" asked Sean.

Amber motioned for them all to come to where she was standing. She then stomped again. The ground beneath her was hollow!

"I wonder if there's a secret tunnel underneath here!" said Dylan.

"Hey! Let's dig the ground up and see if there is!" suggested Kendra.

"Hold it! We can't just go digging up the ground, my Dad would kill me!" exclaimed Amber.

"Then there's got to be a way to get into this tunnel. Maybe a door or something," said Dylan in his smart, logical voice.

"Yeah, but where?" questioned Amber.

Amber turned toward the cellar hole and got an idea. She ran toward it with the other teens running after her. She jumped in and told the others to do the same.

"What crazy idea do you have now Amber?" asked Sean in a slightly nervous voice.

You see, Kendra, Sean and Dylan all knew very well that Amber was a detective and when she's got an idea about a mystery she never gives up and she goes crazy with the idea.

Amber started to knock on the rock wall to see if there was a hollow spot.

In answer to Sean's question Amber replied, "I think this is where the tunnel begins."

"What makes you say that?" asked Dylan.

"Believe it or not, I have heard some pretty strange noises coming from this wall. Like tapping for example," replied Amber.

Sean gave a shudder. Amber found a rock and lifted it out and saw an opening. She told everyone to take out the rocks surrounding the hole. Eventually they found a very large tunnel.

"Wow! This is weird!" exclaimed Kendra.

"Hey, Sean, go get a flashlight in the kitchen," said Amber.

Sean ran to the house and came back in no time at all. He gave her the flashlight and she walked into the tunnel and the others followed behind her. The tunnel seemed like it went on forever. Suddenly they came to an end and found a most startling sight. Dead in front of them was a skeleton of what appeared to be a woman who still had some of her gown on. It must've been very well preserved. The four teens were terrified at this sight.

"Oh my gosh! Look at that necklace!!!" exclaimed Amber.

"That looks like it could be worth a lot of money!" said Sean.

Sean reached for the necklace but Amber stopped him.

"Sean you can't do that! It might upset something or rather someone," said Amber.

"Oh come on Amber! What's the worst that's gonna happen?" questioned Sean with a laugh.

Amber was about to reply when Sean took the sapphire necklace. Suddenly the ground started to shake and the skeleton woman vanished. The teens dashed out of the tunnel and into open sky, which was baby blue, but now turned a threatening color of gray. Lightning struck a nearby tree and thunder roared all around them. The cracks in between the rocks of the cellar hole oozed what looked to be green slime. The teens heard a malicious laugh above them and saw the skeleton woman. She then screeched a name:

"Paul! Paul!!!"

The teens were totally confused. They had no clue about what she was yelling about.

"Ma'am, what is wrong?" asked Sean in a terrified voice.

The skeleton woman swooped down and landed an inch away from Sean. She raised her razor sharp fingers ready to strike when Kendra threw a rock and the skeleton's hand shattered into hundreds of pieces. She screamed really loud and said:

"You all shall vanquish! Let my wrath be upon you all. My people hear me! Attack these foolish children!"

The teens looked all around and saw red eyes glaring at them. When they looked back to where the skeleton lady was she had already vanished. The teens were even more scared for there were ten red-eyed zombies!

"What do we do?" asked Kendra.

Amber gave Sean a look. She was the only one who knew Sean was a master in the martial arts. Amber knew very little after all she was only a blue belt in her karate class. Sean caught her look and he nodded. They both took their positions and destroyed them all until one by one they all vanished. Kendra and Dylan were staring at Amber and Sean in disbelief. Amber and Sean finally told them about their practice in the martial arts.

"We need to get into the house! That's probably the only safe place!" exclaimed Amber.

The rest agreed and they ran as fast as they could to the house.

Chapter 2

The teens got to the house and were deciding how they should fix this problem.

"I told you not to grab that necklace!" exclaimed Amber.

Sean glared at her and replied, "I thought it could be worth a lot of money."

"Well, you thought wrong!!!" shouted Amber.

"Stop fighting! That isn't gonna stop that woman," said Kendra.

"I know, I can karate chop them," suggested Sean.

Amber smiled at that. Then she had an idea, "I got it! We can sneak into the town hall and go into the section where there are old books. That might tell us what and/or who we're dealing with."

"Isn't that dangerous and illegal?" asked Kendra.

"We just gotta be sneaky," replied Amber.

"I'm not so sure about this," said Dylan in an unsure voice.

"Well do you have any other suggestions?" questioned Amber.

Dylan said nothing.

"So everybody ready to go?" asked Amber.

Everyone nodded and they set off for the town hall. Once they got there they were surprised to find that it was guarded.

"I wonder why it's guarded," said Sean.

"I think I have a pretty good idea. That skeleton woman has possessed that man and made him guard this place. She doesn't want us to stop her from taking over."

"Great! So how do we get in now?" asked Sean.

"It's called lying your way in," replied Amber.

This shocked everyone. Amber never lied unless she thought it was truly necessary.

"Here's the plan. I'm going to go sweet talk the guard and I'll have him look away. Then I want Sean to quickly and quietly get the key. Then I'll lure the guard away and you guys go in. When I come back, the key must be in it's place. I'll go around to the back door and you need to unlock it. Then we'll take it from there," explained Amber.

Everyone agreed to this and Amber approached the guard.

"Hello sir. I need your help. I need a strong, tall man to get my cat down from the tree over there," said Amber pointing.

The man followed Amber and Sean quietly took the keys off the wall. He unlocked the door and slowly opened it. The door made a creak and the guard started to turn around but Amber stopped him with, "Sir, please, that cat in the tree needs a tall man like you."

The guard felt proud of himself for that. Sean opened the door a bit further and the three teens walked in. Sean put the keys on the wall and locked the door on the inside. Amber and the guard got to the tree and Amber said, "Oh my gosh! The cat must have been brave enough and jumped down! Sorry about the trouble."

"It's okay, it isn't your fault," replied the guard kindly.

The guard and Amber walked back and Amber said good-bye. Then she walked around to the back of the town hall and Kendra let her in.

"Okay, now we need to be extremely quiet so the guard doesn't become suspicious and catch us," said Amber.

Amber tiptoed to where the old books and documents were kept and took a few books. She gave some books for Dylan to hold and motioned for everyone to follow her out the door. The teens went the long way home so people wouldn't see them taking these old documents.

After several hours they finally reached Amber's house but what they saw was an unforgettable sight.

Chapter 3

In front of them was Amber's house but the skeleton woman's minions were guarding the house and there was no way to get in without being seen. They figured that it'd be best if they went to Kendra's house.

Once they got there they went to the living room and started searching through the books. Suddenly Dylan found something and said, "Hey, check this out! It says in this book that a long time ago this girl named Rebecca, who was about sixteen at the time, had a boyfriend. Her boyfriend gave her this necklace and asked her to become the queen of this evil cult that he was in. She refused which was very unfortunate for her. One night when Rebecca was with her boyfriend Paul, he grabbed her by her hair and dragged her to the tunnel and trapped her there. The legend has it that only her boyfriend's distant relative can release her."

Everyone looked at Sean.

"Kendra do you have a computer or a laptop?" asked Amber.

"Duh, of course I do!" replied Kendra.

Kendra gave Amber her laptop and Amber started typing away.

"Hey, Sean, what's your last name?" asked Amber.

"Saunders. You should know that," he replied.

"Sorry, must've forgotten," said Amber.

After a couple minutes Amber gave a gasp.

What is it?" asked Dylan.

"Apparently the legend is true. Sean is related to Rebecca's boyfriend, Paul Saunders!!!" replied Amber.

Everyone was either jaw dropped or their eyes were wide open.

"So what does this mean?" questioned Sean.

"It means that your life's in great danger," replied Amber sadly.

Sean looked petrified.

"Don't worry, Sean. We won't let anything happen to you," said Dylan.

Sean looked unsure.

"There's gotta be a way to put her to rest!" exclaimed Amber.

"We could try to calmly explain to her that it isn't Sean's fault and we could put her to rest," suggested Kendra.

"Yeah, sure, and get our heads chopped off in the process," retorted Dylan.

"Hey, it's just a suggestion!" yelled Kendra.

"Calm down we don't need to argue now!" exclaimed Amber.

"We need to get to the center of the problem. We need to approach and get rid of Rebecca!" said Dylan.

Chapter 4

All four teens decided it best if they went together to Amber's house. So off they went. Once there they knew immediately that something was wrong. All of the zombies that were there before were gone! The four teens walked carefully into Amber's yard and to the cellar hole and Amber shouted down the tunnel, "Rebecca, I demand that you come out here right now!!!"

A red light showed at the end of the tunnel and Amber knew that was a sign to get out. Suddenly everyone heard a loud high-pitched scream. Out of the tunnel came Rebecca looking angrier then ever.

"How dare you disturb me and speak to me like that!!!" Rebecca screamed.

"Why do you want to hurt us?" questioned Amber.

"One of you has wronged me!!!" she replied.

"We know it was Sean but it's not his fault, it was his 4x great grandfather!!!" explained Kendra.

"I do not believe you foolish children!!" she screamed.

Amber was fed up with this and she held up the sapphire necklace.

"If I destroy this necklace you will go to where you belong, to the other side!"

Rebecca was extremely mad now. She held up her hand and a ball of electricity formed. She threw the ball and aimed for Sean. Sean didn't get out of the way in time but

Amber jumped in front of him and the ball hit her and she fell to the ground with a loud thump.

"Amber!" shouted Kendra.

Dylan held her back when another electricity ball hit the ground next to Amber and Kendra. Kendra ran to Amber's side and took the necklace out of her hand and said to her friends, "This isn't over yet. Not by a long shot."

Kendra got up and faced Rebecca. Kendra held up the necklace and dropped it on the ground. She glared at Rebecca and stomped on the necklace. Rebecca looked furious and along with the necklace, she exploded into a million little pieces. The sky became a bit lighter but it was now evening. Everyone raced over to Amber's side.

"Is she okay?" asked Kendra.

Dylan felt Amber's pulse and replied, "Her pulse is really slow but I think she'll be okay."

Sean and Kendra sighed a breath of relief.

"We should probably bring her to her room or at least somewhere comfortable," suggested Kendra.

The other two agreed and they brought her to her room. After a while Amber regained consciousness and she asked, "Where am I?"

Dylan, Sean, and Kendra got up from their chairs and Dylan said, "You're in your room where it's safe."

"Did we get rid of her?" asked Amber. Sean nodded yes.

"As a matter of fact I got so mad at that spirit that I destroyed the necklace and the skeleton woman exploded into a million little pieces," said Kendra with a smile.

Amber stood up on her wobbly legs and finally got her balance.

"Thank you guys so much for the help! I couldn't have done it without you! You guys rock!" exclaimed Amber.

"Any time," replied Sean.

"So you don't mind helping me?" asked Amber.

"Of course not!" said Dylan.

"So you'd help me again if there's another mystery to solve?" Questioned Amber.

"Duh, just say "mystery" and we're right there by your side!" said Kendra.

"It's great to know that you guys are backing me up," replied Amber.

The others smiled as everyone walked out of the room and down to the living room. "I wonder what other mystery we can solve?" said Amber.

"Oh, Amber! You don't give up trying to find a mystery to solve, do you?" questioned Sean with a chuckle.

Amber laughed and shook her head no.

"Knowing Amber, she'll find one soon enough!" said Kendra laughing.

Everyone started laughing at this but Kendra was right, Amber was going to find another mystery to solve but they didn't know how terrifying this one would be.

The End

Special Thanks To My Friends: Dylan, Sean, and Kendra

The Secret of Camp Mystery

Chapter 1

"Amber Genevieve Oak! Will you calm down?" exclaimed her older brother Chris.

"Ohh! I can't help it, Chris! I'm just so excited! I finally get to be a counselor at the best camp in the world! Camp Mystery!" exclaimed Amber bouncing up and down in the car.

Chris laughed at her and replied, "So you're not worried that you'll have to solve an actual mystery?"

"Of course not! I'm on vacation plus mysteries will just have to wait. I'm gonna help future detectives," she replied with a sure tone.

"You're not afraid that a mystery might sneak up on you?" he questioned.

"No, that's never happened before," she replied defensively.

"Wanna bet? Remember what you told me about your last case the Skeleton's Secret? That caught you off guard."

"Well this time it'll be different. I mean what could possibly go wrong?" she responded.

"Here we are. You got everything?" asked Chris.

Amber nodded as she grabbed her pillow, suitcase and sleeping bag.

"Just be careful, okay, sis?" said Chris in a concerned voice.

Amber smiled and nodded yes.

As she watched her brother drive off she started to wonder about what he said. Would another case sneak up on her or would this be just a vacation? She brushed the feeling off and walked up to her cabin. Once there, she went inside and met her co-counselor.

"Hi! My name is Rheba. You are?"

"I'm Amber Oak, nice to meet you," replied Amber with a smile.

"Wow! I'm so excited to finally be a counselor here," said Rheba.

"Agreed," said Amber.

Amber set up her stuff and glanced out the window at the smallest log cabin she'd ever seen.

"Hey Rheba, who's staying in that cabin over there?"

"Well actually that cabin belonged to the notorious murder/mystery writer. Silvia Forest. She lived there just before she was killed," replied Rheba.

"She was killed?" questioned Amber in shock.

"Yeah, nobody knows why she was killed. I suspect it was just an accident. Well it's a mystery that won't and can't be solved," replied Rheba.

Amber wasn't so sure about that. After all, she has solved mysteries that seemed like they couldn't be solved. Amber forced herself back to reality and just in time too. A camper came in. After an hour, eight more girls were in the cabin.

"Hi girls! It's nice to meet you all. My name is Rheba and this is Amber and we'll be your counselors for the next three weeks! Here at Camp Mystery there will be little hunts to go on and little cases to solve. Amber will hand out the little cases you will be using to solve your mysteries. Now we're gonna head down to the dining hall and we'll have lunch!"

The rest of the day went by very quickly. There were games, swimming, rest time, and finally dinner came.

"Phew, this day went by quick!" exclaimed Amber with exhaustion. Rheba agreed.

After dinner they had another game. This was a mini hunt. The kids really enjoyed running around in the woods. The game ended unfortunately all too soon. Then bedtime came.

Everyone was exhausted, including the counselors.

"Okay girls, now, tomorrow is gonna be a big day so get some sleep and we'll see ya in the morning! Good-night!" said Rheba.

Amber took a shower and put on her pj's. She felt a comforting relief when she slid under the warm covers of her bed and soon fell asleep.

A loud sound awoke Amber from a deep sleep.

"What in the world could that be? Raccoons? Squirrels?" she wondered to herself as she slipped out of bed.

She heard the noise again. It sounded like something was moving around in Silvia Forest's cabin. "I don't think anyone's supposed to be in there!" she thought, as she tiptoed out the door so as to not wake the kids or Rheba.

Amber went over to the window of the lodge and saw a light flicker off the white walls. She peered into the window and saw a person digging through some papers in a big desk. Suddenly a twig snapped from under Amber's foot. The person stopped what they were doing and looked up. Amber ducked just in time, for the person went over to the window and looked out. Apparently the person got the hint that someone might be on their trail so they dashed out the door leaving behind on the ground a piece of paper. Amber went over to the paper and it said, "Find Silvia's Journal!"

Amber took the note and walked back to her cabin.

Chapter 2

The next morning Rheba was awoken by Amber shaking her.

"What's wrong, Amber?" asked Rheba slowly getting up.

"You won't believe what happened to me last night!" she replied with a gleam in her eye.

"Well, tell me what happened?" said Rheba getting up.

Amber related her whole tale to Rheba who seemed quiet.

"Are you sure you didn't just dream it?" asked Rheba who seemed really skeptical now.

"No! I didn't dream it. Someone either at this camp or somewhere near is up to something and I'm gonna find out what!" said Amber with a hint of determination in her voice.

"Well, just be careful Amber, whoever this is might be really dangerous," said Rheba.

"Hey Rheba, how would you like to help me solve this mystery?" suggested Amber.

"I don't know about this, Amber," said Rheba.

"Oh come on it'll be fun. Please?!" begged Amber. Rheba finally agreed and she and Amber started making plans for snooping.

"What would be a good place to start out?" asked Rheba.

"I don't know yet, but let's keep our eyes and ears open for clues," replied Amber. "All right let's go to breakfast," said Rheba.

Amber gathered all the girls together and they all went to the dining hall, but Rheba lingered behind to clean up the cabin a bit. As soon as she was done she went out and started walking toward the dining hall building, but something caught her eye. It was one of the staff members. His name was Tyler Forest. He was tall for his age, which was seventeen, and he always wore dark sunglasses. It always gave him a mysterious look. Unfortunately Tyler wasn't looking where he was going and ran into Rheba, dropping the blankets he was carrying.

"Watch where you're going!" he said angrily.

"Excuse me?!" questioned Rheba.

Before Rheba could say another word Tyler charged off toward the cabins keeping an eye on Silvia's home.

"Hey, Rheba, we're over here!" shouted Amber.

At this point Rheba was red in the face. "Boy, you look mad! What happened?" asked Amber.

"I'll tell you later," replied Rheba through gritted teeth.

Amber understood and went on eating her breakfast.

Later on, while the kids were playing tennis Amber got a chance to talk to Rheba.

"So Rheba, what happened?" asked Amber. Rheba told Amber everything and when she was done she said, "That guy was sooo rude! I can't believe they made him a staff member."

"Maybe he just put on an act, but right now we need to keep close tabs on him," said Amber.

It was around noontime and Amber and Rheba were on their way to lunch and they saw one of their counselor friends Travis Haden. He was also tall and he wore glasses.

"Hey, girls, how's it going?" he called.

The two girls debated on whether to tell Travis what had happened the night before, after all Travis could be a suspect, as well as anyone. They eventually decided to tell him, because he seemed like a nice guy.

"Hey, Travis, we need to talk to you!" exclaimed Amber.

"Shoot," he replied.

The girls yet again related their story and afterward he replied, "I have heard of your sleuthing abilities, Amber, yet again who hasn't, but don't you think it was just a dream?"

"Amber was a bit disappointed and replied, "No. I mean if this was a dream then how did I get the paper?"

"Let me see it," said Travis now becoming interested.

After looking Travis said, "Wow, I guess you were right! All right, I'm in. Tell me what you want me to do."

"Yes! Okay, we now need to follow our suspect without being seen," said Amber.

"Who's the lead suspect again?" questioned Travis.

"Tyler!" exclaimed Amber and Rheba in union.

"Maybe we should split up, like me and Travis will follow Tyler around tomorrow, without him suspecting anything, and Rheba will watch the girls so none of the staff will be suspicious. We will be able to alternate so that way we can watch him basically all the time. So first Rheba will watch the girls and Travis and I will follow Tyler. Then Rheba will take my place and so on."

The other two agreed and Amber and Travis headed off to investigate.

Chapter 3

"So where's the staff cabin?" asked Amber.

"Right over there in the woods," Travis replied.

The two snuck over to the cabin and hid within the trees and waited for the arrival of their suspect.

"Are you sure he's here today?" asked Travis.

"I'm pretty sure he's..." Amber stopped in mid-sentence for Tyler just appeared around the corner with something in his hand.

"What is that he's holding?" Whispered Travis.

"It looks like an old journal," replied Amber.

They could hear Tyler talking to himself. As he got closer they heard him say, "Yes, I've got it! Now just to find Silvia's journal!"

"We should go tell Rheba!" said Travis a little bit above a whisper.

Amber agreed and they ran back to the girl's cabin.

They finally found Rheba taking a walk with the girls along the trail.

"Rheba!!" yelled Amber.

"Did you find anything?" Rheba asked with a hint of excitement.

"Yes, we did, but the mystery got a bit more confusing," said Travis.

"Oh great!" said Rheba.

"Okay, girls, why don't you go play soccer with the other kids," said Amber.

The eight girls ran off to play and all three teens sat down on the side of the hill and discussed what happened.

"So he's looking for Silvia's journal? Doesn't sound harmful," said Rheba. "But don't you think it sounds kind of weird that he's sneaking around in the middle of the night just to find her journal? Why is he so desperate?" said Travis. No one said anything for a while.

"Then you know what we should do right? We need to get Silvia's journal and if at all possible that journal or book he has," said Amber.

"Amber, are you crazy? If we take his copy we're stealing!" exclaimed Rheba.

"Not if we return it! I want to find out what he wants with those journals!" replied Amber with determination.

"You don't give up easily, do you?" asked Travis laughing.

Amber shook her head no. "So when and where are we going to start snooping?" questioned Rheba.

"I want to try in Silvia's cabin, since he was in there before, looking around," said Amber.

"Name the time and I'll be there," said Travis.

"All right, how about tonight at around, say 11:00? That way the kids will be asleep," replied Amber.

"Okay that'll be good. My kids should be asleep too, and if they needed anything my co-counselor will be there," said Travis.

The teens agreed to the plan and they set off to their cabins.

It was 11:00 p.m. and Rheba and Amber were out by Silvia's cabin waiting for Travis. Suddenly he came up running towards them with a look of exhaustion.

"Hey, girls!" he said.

"Hi! Ready to search?" asked Rheba.

"You guys have the key?" questioned Travis.

Amber nodded and took the key out that she borrowed from the office and unlocked the door and opened it.

All three stepped inside and were astonished of how old and beautiful it was. After all, the entire cabin was over a hundred years old. There was a large desk over to the left of them right next to the window. Right in front of them was a large fireplace. To the left side of the fireplace was a little kitchenette, and to the right of the fireplace was a bedroom and bathroom.

"Wow, this place is awesome!" exclaimed Rheba.

The others agreed.

"I want this whole place covered! The bedroom, bathroom, her desk, and near the fireplace," ordered Amber.

"Why the fireplace?" questioned Travis.

"You never know, what if there was a secret compartment that she put her journal in to keep it safe?" suggested Amber.

All three split up and searched the house. Amber went to the bedroom, Travis searched the kitchenette and Rheba searched the desk. After a few moments a scream was heard.

Chapter 4

"Rheba! What happened?" questioned Amber out of breath from running.

"I think I've found what Tyler was looking for!" she replied.

She held up a little notebook with a title of The Forest Family History by Silvia Forest.

"This is so cool!" exclaimed Rheba.

"Yeah... um... girls, celebrate later, run now!" said Travis, with a look of horror in his eyes.

Amber gave Travis a questioning look and asked, "What do you mean?"

"Well, Tyler is on his way here at a fast pace and he doesn't look to happy. He must've heard you scream, Rheba!" said Travis who now turned pale.

The two girls panicked and they all decided to hide near the door. Suddenly the door slammed open and in came Tyler looking more furious then ever! He didn't seem to notice the teens as he ran over to the desk and looked around, "Arghhhh!!" he exclaimed in obvious anger and frustration.

"I need to destroy her book!" he shouted.

"Arghhhh!" he exclaimed again and threw a chair across the room.

The three kids slipped out the door and ran as fast as they could back to safety. They reached the pool area, which was now vacant, and Rheba opened the journal.

"It says here that she grew up with her older brother and she also lived with her mother and father. She started writing at the age of five. Her mother was also a writer and she published a couple books but she wasn't that famous. Unfortunately her father and mother had a huge argument and they divorced. Since then her father was bitter toward her and her brother. He became very temperamental," said Rheba.

"Is that it?" asked Travis.

Rheba nodded.

"We need to find the other journal that Tyler has," Amber said.

The others agreed.

"This is going to be a bit more dangerous, you know. It's in the staff cabin. We'll have to go when everyone's out," continued Amber.

The team decided to go to the male staff cabin the next day during lunch. Then they separated to their cabins and went to bed.

■ ■

"Are you all ready? It's 12:00 and everyone's at lunch," asked Amber.

The rest of the group nodded and they set off for the men's staff cabin. It all seemed quiet and the staff cabin was empty. All three slipped through the door unseen.

"Where do you think his room is?" asked Rheba.

The others had no idea.

"We could split up again," suggested Amber.

"Well, it seems like it's our only option," said Travis.

They all split up and searched the whole cabin.

"Hey guys I've found it, I think," said Travis.

"Wow! This is Silvia's father's journal! Now we have both!" said Amber with excitement.

"Well, thanks for finding Silvia's journal," said a voice behind them.

All three spun around and saw the menacing glare of Tyler!

"I was afraid you'd meddle. Now, Amber give me the books and no one gets hurt," he continued.

"Is that a threat?" she asked advancing toward him.

Tyler advanced toward her as well and replied, "No, it's a promise."

Amber backed up and asked, "What are you hiding?"

Tyler looked more furious and replied, "That is none of your concern!"

Amber quietly and secretively handed Rheba the books and said, "I'm sure you've heard of my abilities of solving mysteries, right?"

"Of course, who hasn't?" Tyler replied.

"Well, there's one thing I attempt not to do," she continued.

"Oh, and what's that?" he asked.

"RUN!!!!!" yelled Amber.

Amber, Rheba and Travis scattered in different directions.

"I warned you, Amber Oak!" screamed Tyler.

"Since when have I ever listened to anyone's warning?" yelled Amber as she ran out the door.

All three made it to safety in the nick of time.

"Is he still behind us?" asked Travis. Amber shook her head no.

Travis opened Silvia's dad's journal and started reading.

"Here it talks a bit about his divorce and he also found out that his daughter (Silvia) started writing, too, and she wrote books and published them. He confronted her one day and they got into a huge argument, so huge he started beating her and it got a bit to far and he um… killed her. He tried to hide it and he did so by saying that she was in a serious accident. Apparently his family was really well known in their town and was looked highly upon. So they had to hide their "good" name from shame!"

"Okay, then why would Tyler want the books?" asked Rheba.

"Wait! Isn't Tyler's last name Forest?" asked Travis.

"Yeah, you're right! What if he wanted to get rid of the books to protect his family's name?" said Amber.

"We should probably put the books back," said Rheba.

"Don't you think her fans should know what really happened? We shouldn't keep it in the dark! It wouldn't be right!" said Amber.

The three teens agreed and then decided to go tell the leader of the camp. He was amazed at their discovery.

"We should alert the police!" exclaimed the leader with excitement as he picked up the phone.

Within a half an hour the police arrived and so did reporters and passers-by.

"So, how did you kids first find this mystery?" asked a reporter who's name was Melissa.

"Well, actually, Amber first suspected something wasn't right. She heard someone fooling around in Silvia's cabin the other day and from there it kind of just flowed into another mystery," said Travis.

"There was also someone who tried to stop us," said Rheba.

"Who would that be?" pressed Melissa.

"That would be Tyler Forest!"

"Oh really?" an officer asked. "He's been wanted by the police for a long time. We've tried to get him for vandalizing, theft, and arson as well. Oh, and look, here he comes now."

After a brief scuffle, the policeman held Tyler while a policewoman handcuffed him.

"We finally caught you, Tyler," said the policewoman handcuffing him.

As they drove Tyler away they noticed a sad look on his face. Amber felt kind of bad for him. He was just trying to protect his families' name, but instead he destroyed it.

"Well Amber, you solved another mystery!" exclaimed Rheba hugging her. "Do you think you'll solve another one?" asked Travis. "Maybe, we'll have to wait and see!" Amber replied smiling.

The End

Special thanks to my friends: Rheba, Travis, Tyler, and Melissa